rai roit

riaume

The
Talking Turnip

ANNE ROSE

PAUL GALDONE
drew the pictures

Parents Magazine Press
New York

To Maria, with love and laughter   A.R.
For Kathleen   P.G.

Library of Congress Cataloging in Publication Data
Rose, Anne K
    The talking turnip.
    SUMMARY: When a turnip, a cat, spoon, and floor
speak to her, an old woman runs off to tell the king.
    [1. Fairy tales] I. Galdone, Paul. II. Title.
PZ8.R654Tal   [E]   79–1144
ISBN 0–8193–1005–0   ISBN 0–8193–1006–9 lib. bdg.

Back then,
when strange things still happened,
a little old woman
lived in a little old house
deep in the woods.

One day she went to cook some soup.
Into a big pot of water
she threw beans and bones
and onions and carrots and salt.

While she was stirring the soup, a turnip spoke up:

"Don't throw me into that boiling water. Leave me alone."

"Who said that?" the woman asked,
looking at her dog.
"That wasn't the dog talking,"
the cat said. "It was the turnip.
Let it be."

The woman was amazed.
Her cat had never spoken before.
Now the turnip and the cat both
talked back to her.

She grabbed her cooking spoon
to whack the cat.

"What?" cried the old woman
as she dropped the spoon
on the floor.

The woman was frightened.
She ran out of the house to tell the King.

On the road she met a woodchopper
with an axe over his shoulder.

"What's your hurry?" asked the woodchopper.
The old woman answered,
"While I was stirring my soup,
the turnip said to leave it alone.
I asked my dog about it.
But my cat said, 'Let it be.'
When I whacked at her with my cooking spoon,
the spoon said, 'Put me down!'
And when the spoon dropped on the floor,
the floor said, 'Pick up that spoon!'
And so I ran."

The woodchopper was amazed.
"What!" he hollered as he flung his axe down.

He ran off with the old woman to tell the King.

Around the corner they met a boy
taking two geese to market.
"What's your hurry?" asked the boy.
"While I was stirring my soup,
my turnip said to leave it alone,"
the woman explained.
"Then my cat said to let the turnip be,
and my cooking spoon said, 'Put me down!'
and the floor said, 'Pick up that spoon!' "
"And then my axe said, 'Did she
pick it up?' " the woodchopper added.

"Is that all?" asked the boy.
"Is that why you're both running?"

"If that happened to you,
you'd run too,"

his geese said.

The boy was amazed.
"What!" he shouted
as he let the geese fly.

The boy ran off with the woodchopper and the old woman to tell the King.

The woman, the woodchopper, and the boy
came to the castle on the hill.

The King sat on his throne and listened to his people's troubles.

At last it was their turn to speak.

"I went to cook some soup,"
the old woman began,
"and everything started to talk to me!
My turnip said to leave it alone,
then my cat said to let that turnip be.
When I whacked at her with my cooking spoon,
the spoon said, 'Put me down!'
And when the spoon fell on the floor,
the floor said, 'Pick up that spoon!' "

"And then my axe said,
'Did she pick it up?' "
the woodchopper added.

"And then my geese said to me,
'If that happened to you,
you'd run too!' " the boy said.

"Now that is really an unbelievable story,"
the King said.
"You'd all better get back to work
before I punish you for taking
up my time with such lies."

The old woman, the woodchopper,

and the boy   all marched out,

but the King sat, lost in thought,
head bent under his splendid crown.
"What nonsense, making up tales
of things talking back to people," he said.
"Foolish troublemakers!"

"Troublemakers indeed!
Who ever heard of
a talking turnip?"

said the King's crown.

About the Author

Anne Rose was born in Antwerp, Belgium, and came to this country as a teenager. In addition to being an art gallery owner and an artist's representative, she has written several books for children and young adults, including the award-winning *Refugee*. Anne Rose lives with her husband and four children in Rowayton, Connecticut. *The Talking Turnip* is her first book for Parents Magazine Press.

About the Artist

Twice runner-up for the Caldecott Medal, Paul Galdone has illustrated over 275 picture books, including several which he wrote as well. Born in Budapest, he came to New York City when he was fourteen and studied painting under Guy Pène du Bois, Louis Bouché and George Grosz. He and his wife divide their time between their homes in New City, New York, and Tunbridge, Vermont. *The Talking Turnip* follows *The Hungry Fox and the Foxy Duck* as Paul Galdone's second book for Parents Magazine Press.